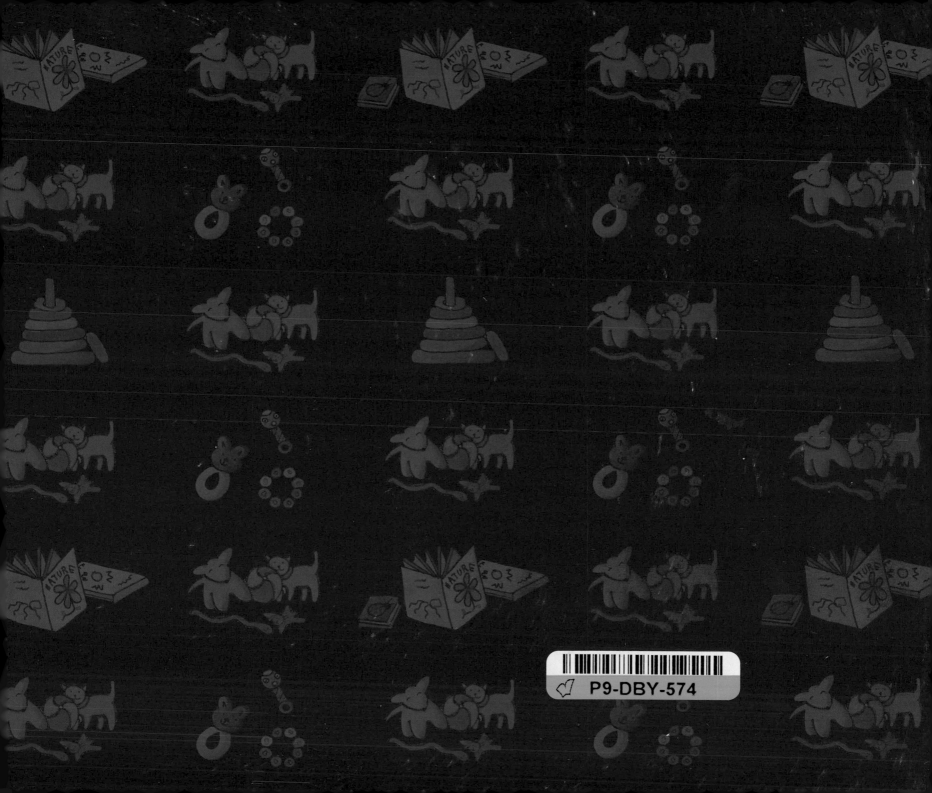

I'm Going to be a Big Sister!

by Brenda Bercun

illustrated by Sue Gross

For my big sister Norene. Forever and ever you will be my big sister.
For my children Ross and Janelle who live the message - BB

For the best big brother and little sister, Sam and Jamie - SG

I'm Going to be a Big Sister
by Brenda Bercun
Illustrated by Sue Gross

The purpose of this book is to educate and entertain.

Pubished by
Nurturing Your Children Press
PO Box 5066
Larkspur, CA 94977-5066

Printed in China by Global PSD
Book design and layout by Jacqueline Domin

ISBN 978-0-9767198-6-1
Library of Congress Control Number: 2005933055

Visit www.nurturingyourchildren.com for additional information.

Dear Parents,

Congratulations on the expansion of your family. The purpose of this book is to support young children in understanding their new role as an older sibling. As the structure of the family changes, it is extremely important for the older child to realize her very essential role.

I suggest that you begin to read this book to your child at the start of your third trimester. Nine months is a long time for a young child to prepare for the arrival of your baby. Once your pregnancy begins to really show, the young child has something tangible to which she can relate.

You are encouraged to use this book to initiate conversations with your child that are relevant to your family. For example, instead of the grandmother coming to be with the child or children, maybe an aunt, uncle, or friend will be the caretaker. Maybe the father is planning to spend the night with the mother in the hospital. Perhaps the new baby and the older child will be sharing a room together. Perhaps you know that the birth will be Cesarean. Maybe you are having twins.

As you prepare yourself and your child for embracing a new life, it is my hope that you find this book and our website a supportive and useful resource for your growing family. Having a positive relationship with a brother or sister does not always come naturally. However, it can be achieved through modeling, understanding, teaching and parental promotion. By reading this book with your child you are taking an important step in the process of promoting a good sibling relationship. I wish you well in your parenting efforts and once again, congratulations.

Best wishes,

Brenda Bercun, RN, MSN
Pediatric Nurse Practitioner
Clinical Nurse Specialist in Child and Family Mental Health
Mommy of Two

Amanda is a wonderful girl. She loves going to the park. She laughs with delight when she swings on the swings.

Amanda has a lot of fun dressing up and playing pretend. Sometimes she pretends to be a doctor. Sometimes she pretends to be a princess. And sometimes she pretends to be a mommy.

One of Amanda's favorite things to do is sit on her mommy's lap while having a story read to her. Mommy's body is changing. Her belly feels hard and is getting bigger and bigger. Mommy's belly is big because inside her body a baby is growing. Amanda is going to be a big sister!

Amanda is noticing other changes happening around the house. Boxes of her old baby clothes are being taken out of the closet. Amanda finds all this activity very curious. Mommy says, "We are getting ready for the new baby. Amanda, you're going to be a big sister."

While reading a book together, Mommy said, "Amanda, put your hand right here on my belly." Amanda felt Mommy's belly move. Surprised, she pulled her hand away. "What is that?" Amanda asked. "That is your little brother or sister moving around. The baby is growing bigger and we can feel it moving." "Mommy, what will happen when the baby gets too big to be inside your belly?" Mommy smiled, "Then it will be time for the baby to be born and you will be a big sister!"

Knock Knock...who's there?

jewelry

One day Mommy and Amanda were cleaning up her room. "Amanda, it's important that you don't let your new brother or sister play with your little toys. Babies like to put everything they can into their mouths. It's their way of learning about their new world. These little toys are too small and a baby can choke on them." "What toys can they have?" Amanda asked curiously. "They can only have toys that are safe for babies."

art supplies

small building toys

board games

SAFE TOYS

stuffed animals

rattles

stacking rings

board books

mobiles

Mommy pulled out a box of safe baby toys. "These were your toys when you were a baby. They are perfect baby toys. They are soft, small enough to fit in a baby's hand, yet big enough so that a baby can't choke on them. If you like, you can give these toys to the baby and teach the baby how to play with them."

soft blocks

"Amanda, since babies like to put everything into their mouths, it's important that their hands and toys are clean. So before anyone touches the baby's hands and toys, they need to wash their own hands, especially after playing outside. It's also important that children only hold and pick up a baby when a grownup is there to help. That way everyone will be safe."

On their way to the store, Amanda wondered about all this baby stuff. How is it going to happen? When is it going to happen? And what does it mean to be a big sister?

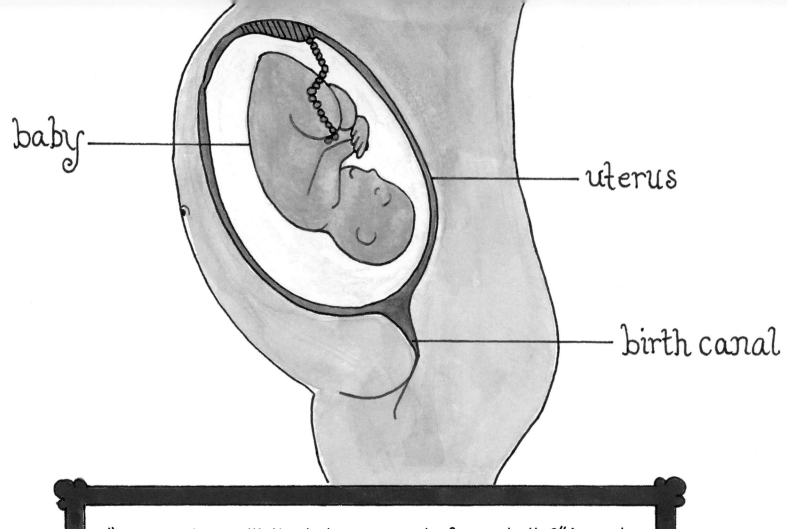

baby

uterus

birth canal

"Mommy, how will the baby come out of your belly?" Amanda asked. "Well Amanda, there's a tunnel in a mommy's body called the birth canal. This is connected to a special place where unborn babies grow called the uterus. When the baby grows too big for the uterus and is ready to be born, it moves through the birth canal. At the end there is an opening for the baby to leave the mommy's body."

While Mommy was unloading the groceries, Daddy came home from work. "Hi Daddy," Amanda called as she ran to give her daddy a hug. "Hi Amanda. How was your day?" Daddy asked as he gave Amanda a swing around. Amanda told Daddy she had been thinking about the baby. After Daddy listened, he invited Amanda to sit down with him and Mommy.

Daddy said, "Amanda, the baby is growing bigger every day." Amanda reached over and touched Mommy's belly. "Mommy and I want to tell you what will happen when the baby lets us know that it is time to come out of Mommy's belly. This can happen at any time during the day or night."

"When it's time, Grandma will come here to be with you and I will take Mommy to a special place in the hospital where babies are born. Mommy may be gone for a couple of nights."

lots of presents

"Mommy and I will call you as soon as the baby is born. When you get the call, you will know that you are a big sister!"

reading

dressing up

art projects

Amanda talked with Mommy and Daddy about all the fun things she will get to do with Grandma. Amanda loves having her grandma come to visit.

cooking

That night when Mommy was helping Amanda get ready for bed, Amanda asked, "Mommy, what does it mean to be a big sister?" Mommy gave Amanda a big hug. "Amanda, you ask such important questions and this question is especially important." Mommy looked into Amanda's eyes. "Being a big sister means being a teacher and an example to your brother or sister. The baby will find you very interesting and will want to look at you, listen to you, and feel your gentle touch. At first, your new little baby brother or sister won't be able to do much because baby muscles are not very strong. The baby will be able to move its arms, legs, and head. He or she will see, hear, smell, feel, sleep, eat, pee, poop, coo, and cry."

"The baby will learn by watching you. When you smile at the baby, you will be teaching the baby to smile. When you talk to the baby, you will be teaching the baby to listen and speak. When you sing to the baby, you will be teaching the baby to sing. In return, you will learn how to be with the baby, how to gently touch the baby, how to understand the baby by the sounds it makes, and how to play with the baby. Your new baby brother or sister will be one of the most special people in your life and you will be one of the most special people in its life. Amanda, being a big sister is a very important job and I know that you will be a wonderful big sister."

twinkle twinkle little star

Amanda began to feel very proud and excited about her new role in the family. She liked the idea of being a big sister and having a new special person in her life to love. There was so much she could teach and show her new baby brother or sister. Amanda reached out to hug her mommy. While they hugged, Amanda felt the baby move. She bent over and kissed her mommy's belly. Amanda couldn't wait to be a big sister.

TIPS FOR PARENTS

1. Include the child when appropriate at doctor's visits to hear the heart beat, etc.

2. Pack a special bag for the child with favorite activities and a special surprise for the time you are away at the hospital.

3. Pick out or make a gift with your child to give to the baby after it is born, and give your child a gift from you for becoming a big sister.

4. With your guidance, allow the child to explore the new baby. Teach gentleness and praise the child's gentle touch.

5. Give language to the baby's different facial expressions and vocal sounds. This will help your child understand the baby and learn social cues.

6. After getting through a difficult day or period of time, acknowledge the challenge and praise your child and yourself.

7. Create special times on a regular basis with the older child to reinforce your relationship with her.

8. When the baby develops new skills such as smiling, etc., praise the baby and compliment the big sister for being a wonderful teacher. "You are an amazing teacher. You are a wonderful big sister. The baby is so lucky to have you and so am I."

9. Children want to please their parents. Gently and firmly redirect inappropriate behavior and strongly reinforce the positive.

10. Strong, healthy families are created by conscious efforts and embracing learning opportunities. **Congratulations!!!**